TALES OF
MY NAUGHTY LITTLE SISTER

My Naughty
Little Sister
Goes Fishing

Dorothy Edwards &
Shirley Hughes

WHSMITH

EXCLUSIVE
· BOOKS ·

A long time ago, when I was a little girl,
I had a sister who was very much younger
than me. Although my sister was often naughty,
most of the naughty things she did were
so funny that no one was cross with her
for very long and she made a lot of friends.

Here is a story about one of my sister's
adventures. It is called My Naughty
Little Sister Goes Fishing.

One day, when I was a little girl, and my sister
was a very little girl, some children came to our house
and asked my mother if I could go fishing with them.
   They had jam-jars with string on them, and
fishing-nets and sandwiches and lemonade.

My mother said "Yes"—I could go with them;
and she found *me* a jam-jar and a fishing-net and
cut *me* some sandwiches.

Then my naughty little sister said, "I want to go!
I want to go!" Just like that. So my mother said
I might as well take her too.

Then my mother cut some sandwiches for my little sister,
but she didn't give her a jam-jar or a fishing-net
because she said she was too little to go near
the water. My mother gave my little sister a basket
to put some stones in, because my little sister liked
to pick up stones, and she gave me a big bottle
of lemonade for both of us.

My mother said, "You mustn't let your little sister
get herself wet. You must keep her away from the water."

And I said, "All right, Mother, I promise."

So then we set off to the little river, and we took
our shoes off and our socks off and tucked up
our clothes and we went into the water to catch fish
with our fishing-nets, and we filled our jam-jars
with water to put the fishes in when we caught them.
And we said to my naughty little sister,
"You mustn't come, you'll get yourself wet."

Well, we paddled and paddled and fished and fished,
but we didn't catch any fish at all, not one
little tiny one even. Then a boy said, "Look,
there is your sister in the water too!"

And, do you know, my naughty little sister had walked
right into the water with her shoes and socks on,
and she was trying to fish with her little basket.

I said, "Get out of the water," and she said, "No."
 I said, "Get out at once," and she said,
"I don't want to."
 I said, "You'll get all wet," and she said,
"I don't care."

Wasn't she naughty?

So I said, "I must fetch you out then," and
my naughty little sister tried to run away in the water
which was a silly thing to do because she fell down
and got all wet.

She got her frock wet, and her petticoat wet, and
her knickers wet, and her vest wet, and her hair wet,
and her hair-ribbons—all soaking wet. Of course,
I told you her shoes and socks were wet before.

And she cried and cried.

So we fetched her out of the water, and we said,
"Oh dear, she will catch a cold," and we took off
her wet frock, and her wet petticoat and her
wet knickers and her wet vest, and her wet hair-ribbons,
and her wet shoes and socks, and we hung all the things
to dry on the bushes in the sunshine, and we wrapped
my naughty little sister up in a woolly cardigan.

My little sister *cried and cried*.

So we gave her the sandwiches, and she ate them all up.
She ate up her sandwiches and my sandwiches, and
the other children's sandwiches all up—and she cried
and cried.

Then we gave her the lemonade and she spilled it all over the grass, and she cried and cried.

Then one of the children gave her an apple, and
another of the children gave her some toffees, and,
while she was eating these, we took her clothes off
the bushes and ran about with them in the sunshine
until they were dry.

When her clothes were quite dry, we put them all back on her again, and she screamed and screamed because she didn't want her clothes on any more.

So I took her home, and my mother said, "Oh, you've let your little sister fall into the water."

And I said, "How do you know? Because we dried all her clothes," and my mother said, "Ah, but you didn't *iron* them." My little sister's clothes were all crumpled and messy.

Then my mother said I should not
have any sugary biscuits for supper
because I was disobedient.
Only bread and butter, and
she said my little sister
must go straight to bed,
and have some hot milk
to drink.

And my mother said to my little sister, "Don't you think you were a naughty little girl to go in the water?"

And my naughty little sister said, "I won't do it any more because it was too wet."

But, do you know, when my mother went to throw away the stones out of my little sister's basket, she found a little fish in the bottom, which my naughty little sister had caught!

My Naughty Little Sister Goes Fishing
Text copyright © 1976 Dorothy Edwards
Illustrations copyright © 1976 Shirley Hughes

My Naughty Little Sister and Bad Harry's Rabbit

Dorothy Edwards & Shirley Hughes

A long time ago, when I was a little girl,
I had a sister who was very much younger
than me. Although my sister was often naughty,
most of the naughty things she did were
so funny that no one was cross with her
for very long and she made a lot of friends.

Here is a story about one of my sister's
adventures. It is called My Naughty
Little Sister and Bad Harry's Rabbit.

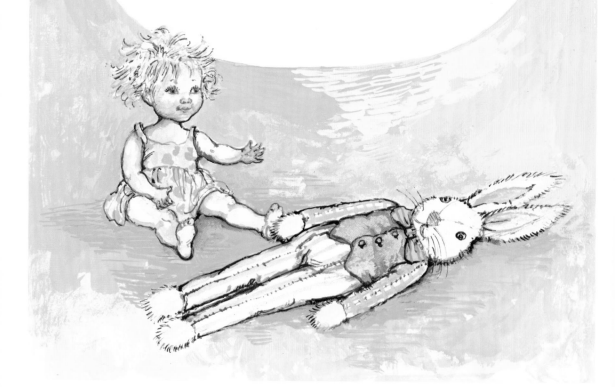

My naughty little sister's friend, Bad Harry, had a toy
rabbit that was nearly as big as himself, and there was a
time when he took it everywhere he went because
my sister took her poor old doll, Rosy-Primrose,
everywhere she went.

When my naughty little sister was tired of carrying
Rosy-Primrose, she would sit her down on the ground,
but Harry's rabbit couldn't sit because its legs wouldn't
bend and when Harry leant it against things, it slid
down, so he had to carry it all the time. My naughty
little sister said Bad Harry's rabbit was a nuisance.

"Why don't you leave it at home?" she would say.
But Harry said he would only leave it at home
if my sister left Rosy-Primrose and my sister said
she wouldn't do that. So as they were very stubborn
children, when they went out Rosy-Primrose
and the rabbit had to go too.

Bad Harry had a kind auntie in Canada who used
to send him presents and one day his auntie sent him
a pair of strong red shoes. It wasn't his birthday
or Christmas—she just sent them!

Harry *was* pleased. "Aren't they shiny?" he said.
"Like red apples."

"Let's try them on," said Harry's mother.
So he kicked off his slippers and stuck out his feet.
But they wouldn't go on. Those shiny red shoes
were much too small for Bad Harry's feet.
Bad Harry couldn't believe it. He kicked and
banged and shouted, but it was no good.

At last his mother fetched his outdoor shoes and
measured the new ones against them and then
Harry saw they really were too small. So he stopped
being naughty though he was still cross.

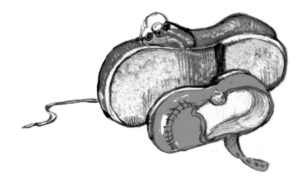

Next day, when our mother and my naughty little
sister came to call for Harry and his mother to go to
the shops, Harry showed them the red shoes. They
certainly were very small. They were even too small for
my little sister and her feet were littler than Harry's.

While his mother was putting her coat on, Harry
fetched his rabbit, and then my little sister had a good
idea. She laid Harry's rabbit on the ground and lifted
up its right foot and she took the right little red shoe
and slipped it on the rabbit's foot and it fitted perfectly.

Then she lifted its left foot, and she took the left
little red shoe and it fitted perfectly too.

Then she stood Harry's rabbit up on
the floor and *it didn't fall over.*

"Look, Harry, he's standing now,"
my sister said, and Harry was
so pleased his rabbit could stand
on its own, that he wasn't cross
any more about the shoes
not fitting him.

"I can stand him up when we're in
the shops or waiting at bus stops now,"
he said.

And that's just what happened. Whenever our mothers stopped somewhere and my little sister sat Rosy-Primrose on the ground beside her, Bad Harry stood his rabbit beside him. Because it was such a big rabbit, all the people going by stared, and stared, and when they saw the red shoes on Harry's rabbit's feet they said, "You are a clever boy," and Harry smiled at them.

Bad Harry liked people saying he was clever, but my naughty little sister didn't. "You're not clever, you Bad Harry," she said. "I'm clever. I put the shoes on, not you."

"He's *my* rabbit," that bad boy said.

Now one of the people going by
was a man with a camera round his
neck, and he lifted it up and took
a picture of Harry and Harry's
rabbit and my little sister and
Rosy-Primrose waiting at a bus stop.

"If I'm lucky I'll get the picture in the paper," the man said, and everyone was very pleased. Harry was so pleased he jumped up and down all the way home and for the next few days he talked and talked about the man taking the photograph and how it would be in the paper if the man was lucky.

And the man *was* lucky and the picture was in the paper and Bad Harry wasn't a bit pleased when his mother showed it to him. There was Harry's toy rabbit standing in the red shoes and Rosy-Primrose sitting on

A little girl with A GOOD IDEA!

the ground and my little sister standing between them
smiling and smiling. *But there was no Bad Harry!*
Under the picture it said: "A little girl with
a good idea."

When his mother read that to him Harry was very
angry. "It's not her rabbit, it's my rabbit!" he shouted,
and when my sister came round to show them the
picture in our paper, in case Harry's mother hadn't
seen it, Harry shouted at her. "It's my rabbit, you
naughty girl! You are in my rabbit's picture."

My little sister had been sorry that Harry wasn't in
the picture too, but when he shouted she stopped being
sorry for him. She said, "Well it *was* my good idea."

After that Harry was so cross and nasty that my little sister picked up the newspaper and went straight home with it and told us how cross Harry was.

"Well, I thought Harry would be in the picture," Mother said. "I remember the man kept saying, 'Keep still, Sonny,' to him. It's a shame, poor little boy," our mother said. Mother was right too, Harry should have been in that picture.

Because my little sister looked so nice in the
newspaper picture, our father went round to the
photographer's shop, to buy a copy to put in a frame.
He brought it home in a big yellow envelope.

Mother was very pleased with it. "What a shame poor Harry wasn't in it too," she said.

Then our father said a funny thing. He said, "Well, it was a rabbit he was taking, not a boy with three heads and six legs!" He took another picture out of the yellow envelope and then he began to laugh and we laughed too.

For there was my naughty little sister and Rosy-Primrose and Bad Harry's rabbit and Bad Harry too, but he had been fidgeting about so much when the picture was taken, that it made him look as if he did have three heads and three lots of legs.

"It was such a good picture the man didn't want to waste it, so he just cut Harry off the end," Father said.

My little sister asked if she could have that picture
to give to Harry and Father said, yes, if she liked,
the photographer had given it to him.

So my little sister took the picture round to Harry
and when Bad Harry saw it he stopped being cross with
her. He looked at himself with the heads and legs and
he was delighted.

"Look at me," he said. "Look at this picture of funny me."

And my sister looked, and Harry's mother looked—and that's just what it was—a picture of funny Harry.

Harry was the *only one you noticed*, for a little boy with three heads and six legs is much more interesting to look at than an old doll, or a standing-up rabbit, or even a naughty little sister.

My Naughty
Little Sister at the Fair

Dorothy Edwards &
Shirley Hughes

A long time ago, when I was a little girl,
I had a sister who was very much younger
than me. Although my sister was often naughty,
most of the naughty things she did were
so funny that no one was cross with her
for very long and she made a lot of friends.

Here is a story about one of my sister's
adventures. It is called My Naughty
Little Sister At The Fair.

When I was a little girl, my little sister used to eat all her breakfast up, and all her dinner up, and all her tea up, and all her supper up – every bit.

But one day my naughty little sister wouldn't eat her breakfast. She had cornflakes and an egg, and a piece of bread and butter, and an apple, and a big cup of milk, and she wouldn't eat anything.

She said, "No cornflakes."

Then my mother said, "Well, eat your egg," and she said, "No egg. Nasty egg." She said, "Nasty apple," too, and she spilled her milk all over the table. Wasn't she naughty?

My mother said, "You won't go to the Fair this afternoon if you don't eat it all up." So then my naughty little sister began to eat up her breakfast very quickly. She ate the cornflakes and the egg, but she really couldn't manage the apple, and my mother said, "Well, you ate most of your breakfast so I think we shall let you go to the Fair."

Shall I tell you why my naughty little sister hadn't wanted to eat her breakfast? *She was too excited.* And when my naughty little sister was excited, she was very cross and disobedient.

When the Fair-time came, my big cousin Jane came to fetch us. Then my naughty little sister got so excited that she was crosser than ever. My mother dressed her up in her new best blue dress and new best blue knickers, and her white shoes and blue socks, but my naughty little sister wouldn't help a bit. And you know what that means.

She went all stiff and stubborn, and she wouldn't put her arms in the arm-holes for herself,

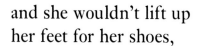
and she wouldn't lift up her feet for her shoes,

and my mother said, "Very well, they shall go without you."

Then my naughty little sister lifted up her feet very quickly. Wasn't she bad?

We went on a bus to the Fair, and when we got
there, it was very nice. We saw cows and horses and
pigs and sheep and chickens, and lots and lots of people.

And there were big swings that went swingy-swing, swingy-swing, and roundabouts that went round and round, round and round. Then my naughty little sister said, "I want a swing! I want a swing!"

But my big cousin Jane said, "No, you are too little for those big swings, but you shall go on the little roundabout."

The little roundabout had wooden horses with real reins, and things to put your feet in, and there were little cars on the roundabout, and a little red fire-engine, and a little train.

First, we watched the roundabout going round and round, and when it went round all the cars and horses went up and down, up and down, and the fire-engine and the train went up and down too. The roundabout played music as it went round.

Then, when it stopped, my big cousin said, "Get on, both of you." There were lots of other children there, and some of them were afraid to go on the roundabout, but my little sister wasn't afraid. She was the first child to go on, and she got on all by herself, without *anyone* lifting her at all. Wasn't she a big girl?

And do you know what she did? She got into the seat of
the red fire-engine, and rang and rang the bell.
"Clonkle! Clonkle! Clonkle!" went the bell, and my
little sister laughed and laughed, and when the roundabout
went round it played nice music, and my naughty
little sister said, "Hurrah. I'm going to put the fire out!"

My little sister had four rides on the roundabout.
One, two, three, four rides. And then my big cousin
Jane said, "We have spent all our money. We will go
and look at the people buying horses."

But my little sister got thoroughly nasty again, and she
said, "No horse. Nasty horses. Want roundabout."
There, wasn't that bad of her?
I'm glad you're not like that.

But my cousin said, "Come along at once," and my naughty little sister had to come, but do you know what she did, while we were looking at the horses? *She ran away.* I said she was a naughty child, you know.

Yes. She ran away, and we couldn't find her anywhere.

We looked and looked. We went to the roundabouts and she wasn't there.

We went to the swings and she wasn't there.

She wasn't at the pig place,

or the cow place

or the chicken place, or
any of the other places.

So then my big cousin
Jane said, "We must ask
a policeman. Because
policemen are good to
lost children."

We asked a lady if
she could tell us where a
policeman was, and the
lady said, "Go over the road
to the police-station."

So my cousin took me over the road to the police-
station, and we went into a big door, and through another
door, and we saw a policeman sitting without his hat on.
And the policeman said, "How do you do, children.
Can I help you?" Wasn't that nice of him?

Then my big cousin Jane said, "We have lost a
naughty little girl." And she told the nice policeman all
about my bad little sister, all about what her name was,
and where we had lost her, and what she looked like,
and the nice policeman wrote it all down in a big book.

Then the kind policeman said, "No, we haven't a
little girl here, but if we find her, we will send her home
to you in a big car."

So then my cousin Jane and I went home, and it was a
long, long walk because we had spent all our pennies
on the roundabout.

When we got home, what do you think? There was my naughty little sister, sitting at the table, eating her tea. She had got home before us after all. And do you know why that was? It was because a kind policeman had found her and taken her home in his big car.

And do you know, my naughty little sister said she'd never, never run off like that again, because it wasn't nice at all, being lost. She said it made her cry.

But, my naughty little sister said, if she did get lost again, she would find another nice policeman to take her home, because policemen are so kind to lost children.

My Naughty Little Sister at the Fair
Text copyright © 1962 Dorothy Edwards
Illustrations copyright © 1979 Shirley Hughes

This collected edition published 1986 by W. H. Smith & Son Ltd
by arrangement with Methuen Children's Books Ltd,
11 New Fetter Lane, London EC4P 4EE
Printed in Great Britain

ISBN 0 416 96820 1